Amara's Encha... Mirror

Unleashing the Power Within

Alex Lockhart

In the intriguing tale of **Amara's Enchanted Mirror: Unleashing the Power Within**, young Amara stumbles upon a mysterious mirror in her grandmother's attic that holds a key to inner strength and resilience. As she gazes into its reflective surface, she utters powerful words: "I am strong, I can do it, and thank you." In an instant, confidence surges through her veins, igniting a transformative journey of self-discovery.

Amara's kindness knows no bounds, and she embarks on a mission to share the mirror's empowering magic with the creatures of the forest. Sensing their loneliness, their yearning to excel in their passions, and their desire for self-belief, she gifts them enchanted mirror pendants. Through her compassionate guidance, Amara encourages each forest animal to look within themselves and repeat the empowering mantra: *I am strong, I can do it, and thank you.*

Amara's forest friends, Louis, Lily, Oliver and Milo embrace the reflective power of the mirror, they awaken their hidden potential and find the strength to overcome their doubts and fears. But it is Catherine, the Sage Owl who imparts the most profound wisdom. With her ancient knowledge, Catherine reveals that the true power lies within oneself. The mirror is merely a catalyst, a symbol that reflects the strength and greatness they already possess. Through the owl's guidance, they realise that their abilities, dreams, and happiness are nurtured from within.

Amara's Enchanted Mirror: Unleashing the Power Within is an interactive, heart-warming tale about friendship, empowerment, and the transformative power of believing in oneself. Teachers, parents and grandparents alike will take pleasure in children joining in with the characters as the powerful words are repeated. A wonderful book inspiring confidence in young minds. Whilst valuing diversity and gratitude the characters in the story realise their hidden potential encouraging readers and listeners of this book to do the same.

Created by Alex Lockhart

Published July, 2023

To my Mother-Always in my heart
Catherine Di Lella, Mary Arghyrou
Louise Hyde & Mary Tilki-Thank You All

EVA & MIA ~ I LOVE YOU

Amara lived in a small cottage with her grandmother on the edge of Whisperwood Forest. Whilst she appeared ordinary, there was nothing much ordinary about her. You see, Amara had a special gift. Amara was extraordinary.

One sunny day, Amara stumbled upon a peculiar old mirror in her grandmother's attic. Through the window, the bright warm sun caught the corner of the mirror as Amara stood facing its wonderous shining light. Curious and excited, Amara touched the mirror, and a magical glow enveloped her.

Amara gazed into the mirror and as she did, suddenly she felt a rush of energy surging through her. She said, "I am strong, I can do it, and thank you." Amara's eyes sparkled with wonder as she realized that she had unlocked a remarkable ability, though she didn't know what it was. Something felt very different from then on, something within. She would soon learn that she could gain extraordinary strength and harness incredible powers simply by looking into the mirror and repeating the powerful words out loud.

That evening, outside the window, was a majestic creature perched atop a tree branch with soft velvety feathers that shimmered in shades of deep blue and silver. It was Catherine, The Sage Owl. Her large round eyes were a piercing amber colour, radiating a sense of wisdom and depth. Suddenly, Catherine spoke and her voice made Amara jump.

Amara, you are stronger than you know, you can do anything you put your mind to!"
Amara still startled replied, "Thanks Catherine, but I wish you would knock on my
door when coming to see me." Catherine replied smiling, "Owls don't knock on
doors!" Amara laughed because she knew that would be ridiculous. Tilting her head,
Amara blinked with a puzzled expression on her face. "Stronger than I know? Really
Catherine, are you sure? I can't lift a car or anything like that!"

Catherine stepped inside and perched upon Amara's hand. The wise owl chuckled softly, feathers rustling as she replied, "Ah, my dear Amara, strength isn't just about lifting heavy things or performing incredible feats. It has to do with your inner strength, kindness to others, and the courage to be true to yourself."

Amara's naughty grin persisted as her eyes widened in comprehension and she nodded. "So, are you saying I have heart power and kindness muscles? Well," said Amara, still not completely convinced, "That sounds pretty cool, I think."

Amara settled for bed peacefully with a smile on her face feeling grateful for the things she knew she had; she had her grandmother and her close friend Catherine. She said to herself, I am strong, I can do it, and thank you. Amara decided to carry small pendant mirrors attaching one to her necklace to keep that magical feeling she had felt close to her heart.

The next morning, Amara spotted a bunny named Louis hiding in the bushes. Louis was nervous and shy to join the other animals in their playful activities. Amara approached him with a warm smile. "Hi Louis, it's fine if you don't want to come out but I would like to show you something." Louis was just the right size for cuddling, not too big, not too small. He had soft fluffy light brown fur and a pink twitchy nose. As he hopped out from behind the bushes, his little tail bobbed behind him.

With a small pendant mirror in her hand, she explained to Louis that this mirror had a unique power to change how he felt. "Louis, look at yourself in here." Louis gradually brought the mirror closer to his face. Louis said, "Wow, it's so shiny!" Excited but impatient, Amara said, "Yes yes but what else do you see, what do you feel? Now say, I am strong, I can do it, and thank you!" Louis repeated the words as he gazed at his reflection in the mirror. Louis's fluffy ears shot up while his little nose twitched in anticipation as he stared into the mirror. A mix of wonder and excitement filled his tiny bunny heart. Later that evening, Louis didn't feel like sleeping and stayed out for hours.

Louis was struck as he had noticed himself standing proud and strong and exuding a renewed vitality and determination, his eyes had widened with excitement. Amara told Louis to wear the pendant as she did. In the days to come, Louis felt the explosion of courage brewing within him. He joined his friends, they noticed that they didn't have to beg him to play anymore. No more hiding in the bushes. Louis's friends scampered as he darted hopping around giggling in the playful game of chase. It reminded him that he was just as bold and brave as anyone else could be, he was ready to explore the world.

Soon Amara met Lily who was a graceful deer with a shimmering coat. She leaped through the forest and dreamt of becoming an artist. However, Lily doubted her artistic talent and feared that her creations would never be good enough. "I just can't get it right, " Lily said. Her canvas stayed blank for much of the time and occasionally she produced beautiful work but felt it was not quite what she wanted to portray. It was always what others told her would be better. Nothing felt like it came from her own imagination.

Amara knew just how to help her. Amara leaned in and whispered, "Believe in yourself and let your imagination guide your brush." She told Lily about the unique power of the pendant mirror she gave her to wear. "Look at yourself and say it Lily, I am strong, I can do it, and thank you."

Lily's paintings became a riot of colours, seemingly chaotic yet filled with a unique beauty that enchanted all who saw them. They saw her art as a reflection of her inner self, bold and bursting with life. Lily's incredible paintings were soon the talk of the forest attracting visitors from distant lands who marvelled at her fearless creations.

Amara felt very pleased with herself but then she remembered Oliver her remarkable and loveable friend who had his own fabulous talents. Oliver a curious forest frog had vibrant green skin and worked hard with an indomitable spirit. He was muscular and could leap soaring great heights with his enthusiasm for athletic pursuits. Lately, he had been sad and given up practising which made him lose his fantastic physique. Amara made him a special sports wrist band that had a mirror encased within the fabric and paid him a visit.

"Oliver, where have you been?"

Oliver replied rather nervously, " Oh, hi Amara, I'm just taking time off, better than failure."

Amara asked, looking very puzzled, "What do you mean Ollie?"

With sadness in his voice Oliver said, "I've given up, I can't do any better and on the last sports day, I even lost the race!"

"You have incredible talent and passion Ollie. Have confidence in your talents and in yourself. Amara reached out and placed a supportive hand on Oliver's shoulder. "You're not alone in this Ollie," Placing the pendant sports band on his wrist, Amara said, "Remember, true champions are made not only through victories but also through the determination to keep going, no matter what." Oliver was humbled by her words and Amara noticed a tear in his eye. "Take this wrist band and look at yourself in the reflection. Say to yourself, I am strong, I can do it, and thank you!"

As time passed, Amara's words became a constant source of inspiration for Oliver, reminding him to embrace the lessons from each setback and to keep pushing himself to new heights. "Practice makes perfect," he said. Oliver wore her gift, he loved the sports band Amara gave him. He repeated the words as he looked at his own reflection in the mirror, I am strong, I can do it, and thank you!" And so, with Amara's unwavering support and encouragement, Oliver found the strength to rise above any obstacle, knowing that even in the face of defeat, his spirit and passion would never be extinguished.

One evening, Amara returned to her grandmother's attic to look into the enchanted mirror again. In the mirror's reflection, Amara was stunned to see a bat behind her in the corner of the attic's vaulted ceiling. She turned to face the scary-looking creature.

"Er, hello, who are you, and what are you doing in my grandmother's attic?"

"I'm Milo; I'm just hanging!"

"Yes, I can see that, upside down!"

"Mm-hmm," Milo responded.

"This is my grandmother's attic! What's the matter with you, are you blind? Oh, I didn't mean…"

Milo interrupted, "No, I'm not blind! In fact, I can see better than you can at night!" Amara laughed, pardon the pun, I know bats aren't blind, you're funny!" Milo was not amused, he said, "Don't you mean weird? Most people think, a bit batty right? Is that what you mean?" "No that's not what I meant," exclaimed Amara, "but you have to admit, when you hide, hang upside down for hours and fly around at night, well it's just different, that's all!" Amara's empathy had created a ripple effect of kindness and understanding.

"You think so? And, I wasn't hiding. Sometimes I can't help but feel lonely. Hanging upside down during the day can be a bit isolating. Actually, if you don't mind, I came to see what all the fuss was about with looking into your mirror, I've been watching you. I was interested in the words you keep saying, so I tried it."

"You know what Milo, I think we have something in common. Just like you, this enchanted mirror has its unique way of standing out." Milo said sadly, "Really? It's hard being unusual, others are afraid of me but I'm different now I've met you." Milo said, "I am strong, I can do it, and thank you. I've always thought the words *thank you* are magical, even the grumpiest people tend to smile on hearing it. Of course, I say it to myself because I am truly grateful for my growing talents too!"

"Remember Milo, the night holds its own magic and beauty. Whilst others are sleeping, you're out there, experiencing a different view that only you can tell others about. Your upside-down adventures bring a touch of whimsy to the darkness; they just don't know you.

"We have a lot more in common than others realise. When others don't understand someone, they sometimes just fear them, it's fear of the unknown."

Milo giggled, "Whimsy? I'm a bat who can see things others could learn from!"

"Absolutely Milo! The mirror reflects your wonderful individuality. You're magical!"

"You know Amara, your words are truly uplifting. Thank you for understanding. It's nice to be reminded that being different is something to be proud of, you are magical too. I can see you have a very special gift. You bring everyone together with your kindness, it has touched my heart," Milo added, "I'll cherish our friendship forever." He laughed, " Ha ha, you can call on me if you get lost in the dark. It's time for me to get ready to enjoy the night, until we meet again then Amara, see you soon!"

The sun set cast a warm glow over the forest. Amara and her friends gathered to celebrate their achievements. They sang out loud and danced. Amara's eyes sparkled with pride. Spirits were lifted by the magic of friendship, gratitude and renewed belief in themselves. Amidst the laughter and music, a familiar figure soared gracefully through the sky. Catherine had been observing their journey from a distance. With a gentle hoot, the beautiful owl descended gracefully, landing softly on a nearby branch.

Silence fell over the gathering as all eyes turned to the majestic creature. "You have all shown great courage and the willingness to believe in yourselves," the owl spoke with wisdom in her voice. "Remember dear friends, the true power and strength lie not in the mirrors, but deep within your hearts." The owl's words resonated in the hearts of every soul present. They realised that the mirrors showed their reflections but the true magic came from within, their dedication to never give up, and their bond of love and support.

Amara stepped forward with emotions of thankfulness and excitement flowing through her. She thanked Catherine for reminding everyone of the precious truth. Amara exclaimed, "Indeed, it is within ourselves that we find the power to overcome any challenge, to embrace our differences, and to create a world filled with love and possibility." They absorbed the forest's charm knowing that its true beauty rested not only in its dazzling hues and glittering lights but also in their unwavering belief in their own powers and the limitless potential that lay within their hearts. Although Amara and her friends realised their newfound understanding was merely another step in their journey, they had formed a wonderful, lifelong kinship. Amara called out, "Let's say it," and before she could finish they sang in chorus together, "I am strong, I can do it, and thank you!"

And so, years later the forest still continues to thrive, as do the spirits of Amara, Louis, Lily, Oliver, Milo and their friends. Together, they embarked on new adventures, facing challenges with courage and a deep trust in their inner strength. And wherever they went, they carried the wisdom of the wise owl in their hearts, forever reminding them that the greatest magic of all could always be found within themselves.